THIS WALKER BOOK BELONGS TO:

_____

_____

_____

_____

For Iona

The Tale of the Turnip
is a traditional English tale retold by Brian Alderson

First published 1999 by Walker Books Ltd
87 Vauxhall Walk, London SE11 5HJ

This edition published 2000

2 4 6 8 10 9 7 5 3 1

Text © 1999 Brian Alderson
Illustrations © 1999 Fritz Wegner

This book has been typeset in Opti Benson Italic.

Printed in Hong Kong

British Library Cataloguing in Publication Data
A catalogue record for this book is
available from the British Library.

ISBN 0-7445-7786-1

The Tale of the Turnip

BRIAN ALDERSON *illustrated by* FRITZ WEGNER

WALKER BOOKS
AND SUBSIDIARIES

LONDON · BOSTON · SYDNEY

*O*nce, a good time ago, there was an old farmer.
He lived in a ramshackle cottage, with a few chickens
and suchlike, and he looked after a few fields.

*B*ut just across the way there was an arrogant old squire, and
he lived in a fancy great house, with stables and gardens, and
fields and meadows, and chickens and pigs, and cows
and horses, and who knows what else.

*N*ow one day the old farmer went
  out into his fields and planted a lot of turnips;

and some of them grew and some of them didn't.

But right bang in the middle of one field there was a turnip that grew ...

and grew ...

and grew ...

and grew ...

and grew.

"*H*en's teeth!" said the old farmer to his missus.
"This is a right champion turnip. We must
take it to the king."
So they got a block and tackle and they
heaved it up, out of the ground
and on to a wagon …

and they took it to the king.

"*Stone the crows!*" said the king. "That's the most champion turnip I ever did see."

He gave the old farmer a cart-load of gold
and the old farmer went home happy.

*W*hen the squire heard about this
he was furious. "What! – What! – What!" he shouted.
"Giving that old codger a cart-load of gold for a miserable turnip!
Why! I've got a stable full of horses out there, and any one of 'em's
worth a thousand turnips. I'll give the king one of those."

So he fetched out his best horse, put it
in the wagon so as not to wear it out,
and he took it to give to the king.

"*By gum!*" *said the king.* "*That's the most poshed-up horse I ever did see. Why — not even the crown jewels are a fit reward for a horse like that. What'll I give you? … I know … you can have …*

my champion turnip!"

The Tale of the Turnip

BRIAN ALDERSON says, "Sebastian Walker is really responsible for this book. Not long before he died, he asked me if I could find any unusual stories in some ancient books in the Opie Collection that I was working on – and *The Tale of the Turnip* grew and grew."

Brian Alderson is a writer, translator and editor. In 1968 he received the Eleanor Farjeon Award for his services to children's literature. Formerly the Children's Book Editor of *The Times*, he still writes for that newspaper. His collection of Hans Christian Andersen tales in translation, *The Swan's Stories*, was shortlisted for the Kurt Maschler Award – as was *The Tale of the Turnip*. He lives in North Yorkshire.

FRITZ WEGNER says, "The wicked humour of this witty tale captured my imagination and to highlight the poetic justice at the end of the story I chose to bring a realistic flavour to the illustrations. Working on farms in my youth helped me to visualize this amazing drama."

Fritz Wegner came to England from Vienna in 1938. He studied at St Martin's School of Art, where he later became a distinguished tutor. He has illustrated numerous books, including *Heaven on Earth*, *The Sneeze* and *The Wicked Tricks of Till Owlyglass* (shortlisted for the Kurt Maschler Award). In 1971 he was awarded the Grand Prix de l'Art Philatélique for his stamp designs. He lives in north London.

Some more classic tales

ISBN 0-7445-3145-4 (pb)

ISBN 0-7445-7223-1 (pb)

ISBN 0-7445-6956-7 (pb)